The Chocolate Cat

By Sue Stainton

Illustrated by Anne Mortimer

KATHERINE TEGEN BOOKS

An Imprint of HarperCollinsPublishers

The Chocolate Cat
Text copyright © 2007 by Sue Stainton
Illustrations copyright © 2007 by Anne Mortimer
Printed in China.

For information address HarperCollins Children's Books, a division of HarperCollins Publishers,
1350 Avenue of the Americas, New York, NY 10019.
www.harpercollinschildrens.com

Library of Congress Cataloging-in-Publication Data
Stainton, Sue.   The chocolate cat / Sue Stainton ; illustrated by Anne Mortimer. – 1st ed.   p.   cm.
Summary: A clever cat helps his owner, a chocolate maker, to discover the magic in his
work and together they transform a colorless town into a place of beauty and happiness.
Includes facts about the history and production of chocolate.
ISBN-10: 0-06-057245-0 (trade bdg.) – ISBN-13: 978-0-06-057245-7 (trade bdg.)
ISBN-10: 0-06-057246-9 (lib. bdg.) – ISBN-13: 978-0-06-057246-4 (lib. bdg.)
[1. Chocolate–Fiction. 2. Cats–Fiction. 3. Magic–Fiction.] I. Mortimer, Anne, ill. II. Title.
PZ7.S782555Cho 2007   2006036101   [E]–dc22   CIP   AC

Typography by Allison Limbacher 2 3 4 5 6 7 8 9 10 ❖ First Edition

To Anne and all chocolate lovers everywhere
–S.S.

To Sue, with love
–A.M.

The old chocolate maker lived alone with Cat.

From a small shop in a small gray village nestled between the sea and the mountains, he made chocolate, like his father and his grandfather before him.

The village was famous for not very much. It was a drab little place.

Cat would watch the window lazily with one eye open, twitch his whiskers, and wait for the shop bell to clang.

But people never seemed to stop for long.

The paint was peeling around the window of the chocolate shop. Inside, the shelves were lined with dusty jars of all shapes and sizes. There were sacks of cocoa beans, some old chocolate-making machinery, and even an old chocolate fountain that hadn't worked in years.

Everything seemed dreary and miserable. But then so was the chocolate maker. Nothing made him smile. He had forgotten how. So people left him alone. Every day more chocolate just piled up in the dusty window.

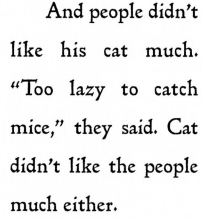

And people didn't like his cat much. "Too lazy to catch mice," they said. Cat didn't like the people much either.

One day, for no particular reason, the chocolate maker made something different. Suddenly there were chocolate mice with crunchy pink-sugar tails everywhere.

The chocolate maker piled the mice high but couldn't be bothered to even taste one. But Cat was

interested. And he thought he saw one move.

Suddenly the pile of pink-sugar-tailed mice tumbled down right in front of Cat's nose. Cat's nose twitched. Wasn't he supposed to catch mice? He gingerly batted and bit a pink-sugar tail.

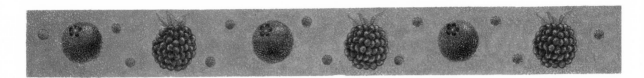

Then Cat tried the chocolate. He could not believe the taste. It made his whiskers and his paws happy.

Then he had an idea. Everyone, simply everyone, should taste this chocolate. Just once!

Cat had a plan.

Cat took the first mouse to the greengrocer's and hid behind the cherries. Mr. Green picked up the pink-sugar tail and took a bite. The taste made him think, "What a wonderful idea!" He ran down to the chocolate shop.

The chocolate maker was grumpy. But in the end they experimented late into the night. Cherries and apricot pieces were soaked in raspberry syrup and covered in the creamiest chocolate, leaving a whole, succulent cherry in the middle. They called them cherry bombs. And soon there were glazed fruits of every kind—mangoes, oranges, pears—dipped in rich, dark chocolate, each even more wonderful than the last, all displayed in the shop window.

The chocolate maker didn't smile, but Cat twitched his nose again.

Those mice were special. Time for another!

The next mouse went to the baker. Cat hid amidst the breads and watched. Mr. Crumb ate his chocolate mouse and chuckled.

"What a brilliant idea!" Within minutes he had clanged the bell of the chocolate shop. And by morning the window was full of Scrumptious Stripes, the tiniest, gooiest cakes striped with thick melted chocolate, topped with white chocolate lace. And soon there were cakes piled high with every combination of chocolates and fruits.

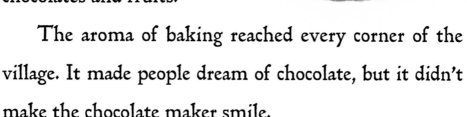

The aroma of baking reached every corner of the village. It made people dream of chocolate, but it didn't make the chocolate maker smile.

Cat's nose twitched again. Perhaps there was magic in those mice. Time for another!

The next mouse went to the delicatessen.
Cat hid among the spices.

Mrs. Hazel ate her chocolate mouse, then skipped
to the chocolate shop, singing, "What an amazing
idea!" By morning the window was
full of chocolate slabs so large you had
to break them with a hammer, piled high with nuts,
honey, and exotic spices. And soon there was scented
Turkish delight in every shade of pink and
green and jugs of thick, steamy hot chocolate.

It was enough to make your mouth
water. Just by looking.

But none of it made the chocolate maker smile.

Cat licked his lips. There was definitely magic in
those mice. Time for another!

The next mouse went to the flower shop. Cat hid behind the roses.

Mrs. Bloomer ate her chocolate mouse and giggled. "What a beautiful idea!" She left trails of flower petals all the way to the chocolate shop. And soon there were chocolates with real, crystallized violets and primroses, and rose-petal jellies with real rose petals. The scents were extraordinary.

And now outside the shop were baskets of violets with lemon-scented geraniums and pink roses.

All the colors and scents made the chocolate maker's head spin, but they did not make him smile.

The aroma made Cat dizzy. He thought he saw chocolate mice everywhere. Time for another!

PRALINE NOISETTE

CHOC

The next mouse went to the hardware store.

Cat hid behind the saucepans.

Mr. Steel ate his mouse and laughed.

"What a fantastic idea!" He clattered and clanged down to the chocolate shop. And soon there were chocolate stars and moons. From tin molds they made chocolate fish, rabbits, and hens. The chocolate fountain was repaired.

Chairs and tables were set outside among the flowers. And people came and sipped hot chocolate. Then the chocolate shop was painted.

But still the chocolate maker did not smile.

Cat couldn't believe his eyes. What next!

"Niice magic miices, magic miices niice," Cat sang.

Then children started coming by and suggesting ideas. The chocolate maker was inspired. He made fat, twirly aliens with green jelly middles, puffy pink pigs, and honeycomb fireworks that would sparkle in your mouth. Then there were chocolate pebbles that would last forever and apricot clouds that would melt on your tongue.

Now everyone was talking to the chocolate maker! And he was talking to everyone else. But he still didn't smile. Not once.

Sipping hot chocolate seemed to make the people relax, gossip, and watch the world go by. They even talked to Cat. Cat could not believe his ears. He even began to quite like everyone.

The chocolate maker would gaze at all his creations proudly for hours. Then, one day, he saw a chocolate mouse move.

He caught the mouse by the tail and suddenly could not resist a taste. The taste traveled all the way from his head to his toes to his fingers. And then, of course, he had an idea! A wonderful, brilliant, amazing, beautiful kind of idea!

Cat hid behind the pile of mice, considering his cleverness. He waited.

The chocolate maker started working. And he worked for a long time.

The chocolate seemed to come alive as the chocolate maker worked. Almost magically, the chocolate, dark and white, turned into wondrous sculptures. He told Cat stories about them. Cat watched, listened, and wondered what would come alive next.

Then, quite suddenly, the chocolate maker smiled!
And he laughed until his toes twiddled. The more
he laughed, the more the chocolate became whatever
the chocolate maker imagined. Ferocious fiery dragons,
sailing ships, and turreted castles. They were all much
too big and wonderful to eat!

Cat smiled too. At last!

*A*nd now the village was famous. A faint aroma of chocolate and spices hung in the air. It made people dream of chocolate.

And people came from far and wide to see the chocolate maker work, but the sculptures hidden deep inside the chocolate shop were always a surprise. And in the window, made from the darkest chocolate, was a magnificent sculpture of Cat. Smiling.

Every now and then Cat is still given a chocolate mouse. But not very often because, as you know, you should never eat too much of scrumptious things.

Because they lose their magic.

Chocolate made with real cocoa butter and a high cocoa content is actually good for you! Sadly, though, it is not always easy to find.

It all started in the last millennium B.C.E. with the Olmec and the Maya, who believed the cocoa tree to be a gift from the gods and cocoa to be the food of the gods. Later, the Aztecs used cocoa flower and the bark as medicine to cure all sorts of illnesses, everything from shyness to depression. They made a drink called xocoatl from grilled, ground cocoa beans, pimento, and corn flour. Vanilla and chili pepper were also often used. The Aztec emperor Montezuma was reputed to drink fifty goblets of xocoatl a day. Later, with the addition of ginger and other spices, the drink was thought to have magical properties.

When the Spanish conquistadors landed in Mexico in the early sixteenth century, they were presented with large quantities of cocoa beans. They didn't like the drink. But the beans had great value and were, they say, traded—four beans for a pumpkin, ten beans for a rabbit, and one hundred beans for a slave. Cocoa beans and the drink recipe were taken back to the Spanish court and kept secret for nearly a century. But the secrets of cocoa eventually passed throughout the courts of Europe. By the end of the seventeenth century, the cocoa drink was considered a luxury item among the nobility.

The first chocolate was prescribed as a medicine to prolong life. Chocolate does contain B vitamins as well as iron and other minerals.

Cocoa pods are picked from trees. The beans are taken from the pods, covered, allowed to ferment, and dried. Then they are roasted, the husks removed, and the insides crushed and ground to make cocoa paste. Cocoa butter is extracted from this. The mixture is then kneaded with sugar and milk and refined to make it smooth and less bitter. Then it is cooled, molded, and packed. And, of course, eaten. . . .

Plain chocolate contains cocoa paste, cocoa butter, and sugar. Milk chocolate contains cocoa paste, cocoa butter, sugar, and milk. White chocolate contains cocoa butter, sugar, and milk.

A note: It is not a good idea to feed your cat chocolate mice, as it may make him or her sick. But real mice are fine.